SPIKE!
The Hedgehog
Who Lost His Prickles

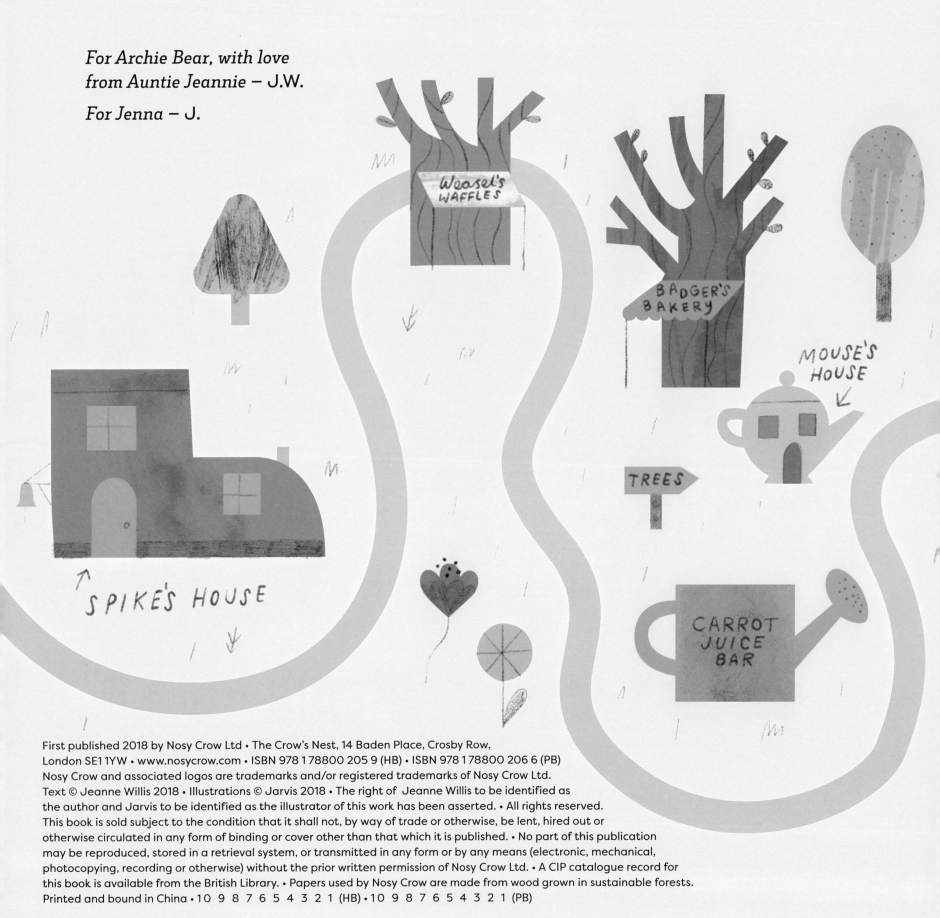

For Archie Bear, with love
from Auntie Jeannie – J.W.

For Jenna – J.

First published 2018 by Nosy Crow Ltd • The Crow's Nest, 14 Baden Place, Crosby Row,
London SE1 1YW • www.nosycrow.com • ISBN 978 1 78800 205 9 (HB) • ISBN 978 1 78800 206 6 (PB)
Nosy Crow and associated logos are trademarks and/or registered trademarks of Nosy Crow Ltd.
Text © Jeanne Willis 2018 • Illustrations © Jarvis 2018 • The right of Jeanne Willis to be identified as
the author and Jarvis to be identified as the illustrator of this work has been asserted. • All rights reserved.
This book is sold subject to the condition that it shall not, by way of trade or otherwise, be lent, hired out or
otherwise circulated in any form of binding or cover other than that which it is published. • No part of this publication
may be reproduced, stored in a retrieval system, or transmitted in any form or by any means (electronic, mechanical,
photocopying, recording or otherwise) without the prior written permission of Nosy Crow Ltd. • A CIP catalogue record for
this book is available from the British Library. • Papers used by Nosy Crow are made from wood grown in sustainable forests.
Printed and bound in China • 10 9 8 7 6 5 4 3 2 1 (HB) • 10 9 8 7 6 5 4 3 2 1 (PB)

SPIKE
The Hedgehog
Who Lost His Prickles

Jeanne Willis & Jarvis

AIRPORT

MOLE'S HOUSE ←

THE LEAKY LAKE

↑ THE BIG OLD TREE

nosy crow

Spike the little hedgehog was as **prickly** as can be.
He went to bed with prickles on as you can clearly see.

BUT . . .

in the night, he had a **fright** – he dreamt about a **fox!**
A scary dream in which he had a **lot** of nasty shocks.

So, filled with fear and trembling, he woke up with a shout.
Then, "Eek!" he saw he had no . . .

...PRICKLES!

They had fallen **out!**

He hardly recognised himself,
all spineless, soft and pink.

"I'm in the **nude**. How **rude!**" he blushed.
"What will the neighbours think?

I need something to **wear**," said Spike,
"to stop me looking silly."

So he wore a paper lampshade,
which was white and rather frilly.

"Ah, this will do the job," he said. "I can go out again.
No one will see I'm prickle-free . . ."

Then it began to rain.

It rained upon the lampshade and . . .

. . . it made the paper **tear**.
"Look at Spike!" the rabbits laughed.

"He is completely **bare**!"

CARROT JUICE BAR

"Please don't **stare**," Spike mumbled.
"Does my bottom really show?"
"You have no prickles!" they replied.
"You're **bare** from head to toe!"

THE
WOODS →

Spike was **most** embarrassed
and he ran off through the wood
to find another thing to wear.
(That lampshade was no good.)

He found . . .

. . . a picnic basket with a **china plate** and **cup**,
and wore them like a **hat** and **coat** to keep him covered up.

Off he went, quite confident his
bottom **wasn't** showing . . .

but as the cup fell past his eyes,
he cried, "Where am I going?"

The china **smashed** to pieces
as he crashed into a tree.

"You're all **bare!**" barked Badger.
"You have **nothing** on, I see!
Hedgehogs should have prickles!"
Badger snorted. "Where are **yours?**"

AIRPORT

Spike scuttled off and muttered that
he'd left them back indoors.

But on the way, he found . . .

. . . a holey **sock** beside a stile.

"I'll wear it like a **smock!**" said Spike
and gave a little smile.
"It fits me **perfectly**," he said,
"and hides my knobbly knees.
No one will guess I'm prickle-less . . .
although it stinks of **cheese.**"

So, warm and fully woolly,
he went on his **merry** way,
wishing all the animals he met a lovely day.

THE BIG MATCH
FOX CITY
v
OWL UTD

THE TREE TOP TIMES

NO MORE NUTS

THE LEAKY LAKE

But to his great dismay . . .

. . . the sock **unravelled** on a thorn.
"You're all **bare**," teased Weasel,
"as the day that you were born!"

"Oh, please don't **tease** me, Weasel!"
little Spike said with a sigh.
"I don't know why I have no prickles
and it makes me **shy**."

But Weasel said, "You'll **freeze**!
A chilly breeze is in the air.
You'll catch a cold and **sneeze**,
so please put on some underwear!"

Spike went red and off he fled. He had no pants or vest.
He really missed his prickles and felt badly underdressed.
And just when he believed he couldn't bear it any more . . .

. . . he saw **balloons!** A great big **bunch!**
Attached to Mole's front door.
Spike grabbed the string.
"They're just the thing to cover me," he said.
And he wound balloons around himself
from tiny toe to head.

"The **height** of fashion!" Squirrel said.
"So colourful and round!"

BUT . . .

as everyone **admired** him,
Spike **lifted off the ground!**

He drifted, shifted by the wind,
and floated out of sight . . .

The sun went down.
Away he blew into the moonlit night.

Over snowy mountains where the **wild** grey wolves all howl . . .

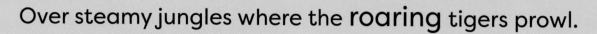

Over steamy jungles where the **roaring** tigers prowl.

Twice around the world he went.
He thought he'd **never** stop.

Then he saw his **home!**

He waved.

And his balloons went . . .

He dropped down to the mossy ground
and landed . . .

. . . with a **thud.**
The burst balloons, in tatters,
scattered round him in the mud.

"Spike's **not** bare!" his friends declared.
"He's sharper than a tack!"

"I popped all my balloons!"
whooped Spike.
"My prickles have
grown back!"

So Badger threw a **party** for him – everybody came!
Prickly Spike **no longer** had to hang his head in shame.

And even when he turned to leave,
his friends were **very** kind, pretending not to see the . . .

. . . cupcake **stuck** to his **behind!**